D0293145

For Joe, who isn't afraid of anything — R.L.

Text copyright © Rebecca Lisle 2000
Illustrations copyright © Peter Dennis 2000

Published in Great Britain in 2000
by Hodder Wayland, an imprint of
Hodder Children's Books

A catalogue record for this book is available from
the British Library.

ISBN: 0 7500 3005 4

Printed in Hong Kong by Wing King Tong

Hodder Children's Books
A division of Hodder Headline Limited
338 Euston Road,
London NW1 3BH

REBECCA LISLE

The Empty Grave

Illustrated by Peter Dennis

HODDER
Wayland

an imprint of Hodder Children's Books

Chapter One

They say that you can't touch a ghost, that ghosts have no substance. But listen, I know that's not true, because I *have* touched one. You don't believe me? Well, let me tell you about it...

It all happened last summer when we went down to help Aunt Judy and Uncle Bill renovate an old house in Dorset. They planned to turn it into a holiday guest house, but of course they didn't know it was haunted then.

The place was called Gulliver House and it was beautiful. It had honey-coloured stone walls covered with climbing ivy and roses, and lovely gardens with tall, old trees.

My cousin, Freddie, greeted us with cries
of delight. "Hello, everyone – Jay, it's great
to see you!" he yelled. "Look at this place.
Isn't it brilliant? We're all going to sleep in
the attic."

"Where's the loo?" I asked Freddie as we
went inside.

"There was one down here," he said,
giggling, "but the old chain came off in my
hand! Go up those little stairs at the back,
turn left, then you'll see the other one."

I ran up the bare, narrow staircase and
Jolly, my dog, scampered up behind me.

At the top of the stairs I turned left down
two little steps. In front of me was a corner
and a tiny window that looked down towards
the river.

Then I stopped. Jolly stopped too. She
whined quietly.

Suddenly goose bumps erupted over my bare skin, first on my arms and then they trickled up my arms to my neck and all over my head and down my back. Jolly spun round and ran downstairs, her nails clattering on the bare wood.

Something had really scared her – and me – and yet there wasn't anything there. Just a little window. A narrow corner in the corridor.

We're just spooked because it's an old house, I told myself. I didn't think anything more of it, until later that night.

Freddie, Millie and I lay on mattresses in a line along the attic floor. There were low windows along one side and we could lie on our tummies and look out into the garden which was still dimly lit by the evening sun.

"I'm really glad you two are here," said Freddie. "Mum and Dad won't admit it, but this place is so spooky!"

Millie shivered and snuggled further down into her bed. "Don't," she giggled.

"What's spooky about it?" I asked, suddenly suspicious.

"Mum says the house is *unhappy* – typical Mum. After we'd bought it, the estate agent said it might be haunted! Now, don't laugh, but I do get this really funny feeling at the top of the back stairs—"

"Just by the bend where the tiny window is?" I interrupted.

"Yeah! How did you know?"

"Because I got it too!"

"Now that *is* spooky!"

"Jay, are there such things as ghosts?" asked Millie.

"Oh, *no*! No such thing and certainly not here," I told her, winking at Freddie. I didn't want Millie spooked, she was only six. "Don't you worry."

I hoped I sounded really confident, but I didn't feel it.

Chapter Two

The next day Freddie showed us around.

Behind the house there was an old church and a river. The river looked fast and deep and dangerous as it swished past.

A gate in the garden wall led into the churchyard, and we went in. An old man was snipping at the long grass with shears and we waved to him.

"Look," I said. "Here's an odd grave."

It was a very old tombstone, with a strange-looking angel perched on the top. On the stone there was some writing which said:

"Edwin Mortimer Gulliver
June 4th 1839
There is no body to lie below
There is nowhere for him to go
He shall always stay with me
This is the way it was meant to be."

"That gives me the heebie-jeebies," said Freddie, shuddering.

"I want some heebie-jeebies, too. What are they?" asked Millie.

Freddie and I grinned at each other.

"Why don't you pick us some daisies instead?" I said.

"OK, Jay."

Suddenly a long shadow fell across the grave. It was the old gardener.

"You're the new folk from Gulliver House, aren't you?" he asked, leaning on his spade.

We nodded.

"Didn't take you long to find out about him, then," he said, nodding at the grave. "Has he been giving you trouble already?"

"What do you mean?" asked Freddie.

"Why, that Edwin," the gardener said. "He lived in Gulliver House, he did. That's his grave, where he should be. *Only he's not.*"

"What do you mean he 'should be' in the grave?" I asked.

"Well," said the old gardener, "see, it says there was no body, doesn't it? He was drowned right here in the river and he was laid out dead on the grass. Put in a coffin. Then he disappeared. They say his mother wept for three whole years. He was her only child, you see, and such a beautiful boy. She blamed herself for his death and couldn't get over it. His body was never found. He was never laid to rest, see, so he haunts the old house and always will, until someone finds him."

"That's horrid," said Freddie, turning pale.

"Aye. Dreadful. *Awful*," said the gardener. "And you'll try and make that old house look nice and you might even manage, but you'll never get rid of the sadness. No point in trying, I say."

Slowly, we went back to the house.

"I wish he hadn't told us that story," I said.

"So do I," said Freddie in a strangled voice. "So that's why the place was cheap, because everyone round here's frightened."

"Frightened of what?" asked Millie, returning with a handful of daisies.

"Er... nothing," I said.

Back at the house, Mum and Aunt Judy were painting the hall. We could hear Uncle Bill hammering in the kitchen.

"Come and help," said Aunt Judy.
"Freddie, you can get some more brushes.
Jay, run up and find some old clothes for
you and your sister."

Ladders and paint pots were blocking the
top of the main stairs, so I ran through to
the narrow stairs at the back and just as I
rounded the funny corner, a marble came
rolling along the floor towards me. It
bounced over the uneven boards and
rolled to a standstill at my feet.

I picked it up.

It was an old marble, made from creamy-coloured glass with a strange purple whirl in the centre. I closed my fingers round it. Immediately those goose bumps came back, like tiny pins pricking out through my skin. I shuddered.

"Is this yours?" I asked Freddie, showing him the marble.

He shook his head.

"No. I've never seen it before. I don't play with marbles and anyway, that one's really old."

Chapter Three

I woke up in the middle of the night.

I could hear a child crying. But who?
Where? Millie and Freddie lay fast asleep
beside me. Something weird was going on.
Do ghosts cry? I wondered. I should have
been worried then, but more than anything,
I wanted to try and help.

I crept out of bed and went to the top
of the attic stairs. I went slowly down the
twisted staircase and stopped at the bottom.
The sobbing was close by.

I walked gingerly along the corridor,
stepping in and out of the streaks of silver
moonlight until I came to the corner where
I'd got the horrid shivers. Of course, *of course*
– the noise was coming from there. It was as
if the wall itself was crying.

"Don't!" I called out. "Please don't cry!
It'll be all right. I'll find you."

Immediately, the sobbing stopped. I put
my hands against the old wall as if I was
trying to comfort it and suddenly, under
my fingers I felt something... a doorway?
I reached up and across. Yes, it really was
the rough shape of a doorway. There had
to be a room there. A hidden room.

Suddenly I felt frightened. I ran to Mum's room. I thought I was going to tell her, but...

"What is it? Jay, is that you?" she asked.

"I had a nightmare," I cried, flinging myself into bed beside her. "I need you."

"I know," murmured Mum. "It's hard to sleep in a strange house."

I was too tired to argue. Soon we both fell asleep.

Chapter Four

The next day I told Freddie about the crying and the hidden door.

"You heard the ghost of the drowned boy *crying*?" Freddie squeaked. "Weren't you scared? You are brave. You should have woken me, I'd have come with you!"

"Would you?"

"Of course! Hey, ghosts don't come out in the daytime, do they? Come on, let's go and look! If we find where Edwin was hidden, we might stop the place from being haunted."

"Yes. Listen, I've got a hunch," I told him. "Come outside."

We looked up at the small window in the corridor that looked out over the river. Thick ivy grew all around it.

"There, Freddie!" I shouted. "I knew it! There's another window beside it, under the ivy. I bet you don't know which room *that* belongs to."

Freddie scratched his head.

"I'm sure there isn't a room there!"

"See, I told you. It's the *ghost room*!"

Just then Millie ran up to us.

"Look what I've got!" she said, holding out a little leather bag.

"What's that?" I asked.

"Just my marbles," she told me. "Want to see?"

Marbles?

Millie poured the creamy-coloured marbles into my hand. They were just the same as the one I'd found.

"Where did you get them?" asked Freddie, trying not to look worried.

"From that little boy," said Millie.

"Which little boy?"

"Oh, you know, the one with funny old clothes on," said Millie. "That velvety jacket and shoes with buckles. He's nice, but he's very lonely. No one knows where he is. No one ever comes to see him."

I shuddered. "What's his name?"

"Edwin," said Millie. "And he was so glad to see me. I told him I was lonely sometimes, too. He wanted to play so I played and then he gave me these," and she skipped off to show Mum the marbles.

"Oh, heck," said Freddie. "Edwin? That was the boy's name, wasn't it? Jay, your sister's been playing with a ghost!"

I didn't know what to do. "Should I tell Mum or Uncle Bill?" I asked Freddie.

"No, they'll never believe us. But we've got to tell them about the hidden room."

Of course, the grown-ups thought we were wrong to begin with, but Uncle Bill soon had to agree that there was a blocked-off doorway.

"How exciting!" said Aunt Judy. "But we won't start undoing it now. We've got so much else to get on with, tomorrow will be soon enough."

A pity. We could have saved ourselves from a long night of worrying if we'd done it there and then.

Chapter Five

Freddie woke me in the middle of the night.

"Millie's gone," he said. "I'm scared."

Somehow I knew she hadn't just gone to Mum. She was with Edwin.

We dashed downstairs as quickly and quietly as we could and scrambled into wellington boots then out into the garden.

"There!" I yelled, pointing to the river path.

Millie's white nightie shone brightly in the moonlight. She seemed to float above the ground as if it wasn't really there. Beside her, holding her hand was a smaller, darker figure.

Edwin.

"Millie! Millie!" we called, but she didn't seem to hear us.

I chased after them, but my wellies were too big and I skidded. I tried to grab at Millie, but my outstretched fingers only touched Edwin.

Just for a moment, his icy little hand touched my living flesh and it was as if a thousand tiny electric icicles were piercing my skin. It sent tremors up to my scalp and down to my toes.

The ghost turned and smiled at me.

"I just wanted someone to find me," he said softly. "Can you find me?" And then they were gone.

We looked everywhere. We ran inside and up to the attic. We searched every room.

Nothing.

Where? *Where?* I wondered. Then I knew.

"He's got her in there! In the ghost room. The blocked-off room. She'll never get out!"

Suddenly Mum and Uncle Bill and Aunt Judy appeared. Millie's empty bed and the little bag of marbles forced them to believe our story.

"You've got to knock down that wall!" I told them. "Millie's in there. She may be in danger!"

"But there's no such thing as ghosts. *Is there*?" said Mum, uncertainly.

"Come *on*!" I was close to tears. "Hurry!"

Uncle Bill looked grim. He rubbed his fingers over the hidden doorway. "It's worth a try."

So we began ripping off the wallpaper and tugging at the plaster, and in a few minutes we had reached the bricks and Uncle Bill was thwacking at them with a sledge hammer.

"Millie! Millie! Are you there?" cried Mum.

At last Uncle Bill was through, and we pulled at the remaining bricks and went in.

It was absolutely amazing.

The room must have been exactly the same as it was when Edwin died, all those years ago. There was a small iron bed, lace curtains, a washstand and a rocking horse. There were lead soldiers all laid out ready for battle, marbles in a dish and a wooden skittles set. Lying on the bed was Millie.

"Millie!" cried Mum, rushing over to her.

Millie opened her eyes. She smiled at Mum then looked around. "Oh, he's gone," she said sadly.

"Who?"

"Edwin. He said he couldn't come out again, unless I came in. Do you know, Mum, no one had been in here for ages and ages. He'd been forgotten. He said you'd come looking for us and you did. I think he'll be all right now," said Millie. Then she turned over and went straight back to sleep.

I told Aunt Judy the whole story. "The gardener at the church said Edwin was drowned and then disappeared. Why do you think he was locked up in that room?"

"My guess is his mother couldn't bear to be apart from him," said Aunt Judy. "Remember, he was her only child. They must have been very close. She couldn't let him go and so she kept him here. I can understand that... But he was lonely in there all these years, poor little thing."

"I heard him crying," I told her. "But I don't think I will again."

"No," agreed Aunt Judy. "I think the ghost of Gulliver House has gone."

Chapter Six

Millie was very pleased with herself in the morning, she loved all the attention.

"But how did you get into that room?" I asked her.

"Well, it was odd," said Millie. "When I held his hand everything went faint and fuzzy. I couldn't see you. We ran into the house and it was all old-fashioned and dark and then we went into his bedroom..."

"Through the door?" I asked.

"Of course!"

"You went back in time!" cried Freddie.

"I did not!" giggled Millie.

But I think she had.

"He said you'd find us," she added. "He said it was the only way and then I held his hand so he could go to sleep, and he did."

Freddie and I found the funny feeling had
gone from the corner in the corridor. It was
disappointing in a way.

"It's not haunted now," said Uncle Bill.
"Not that I really think it was, of course,
but it feels happier, doesn't it?"

Then we went back to the graveyard,
and that was a happier place, too, because
Edwin's gravestone had changed.

Here lies the body of
Edwin Mortimer Gulliver
Sleeping safely with the Angels
June 4th 1839

Millie still didn't believe in ghosts.

"But Edwin wasn't a ghost," she said.
"Don't tease me. You said there was no
such thing, and I believe you, Jay."

I didn't say anything. After all, I'd touched
Edwin and it was something I would never
forget. I knew. I knew for certain...

Ghosts really do exist.

DARE TO BE SCARED!

Are you brave enough to try more titles in the Tremors series? They're guaranteed to chill your spine...

Picture of Evil by Sam Godwin
When Rachel finds an old portrait, strange things start to happen. Why does Rachel feel tired all the time? And why does the woman in the picture seem to be getting younger? There could be more to this portrait than meets the eye...

Beware the Wicked Web by Anthony Masters
In the dead of night, Rob and Sam explore the forbidden attic at the top of their new home. When they find a sprawling, sticky web, with a giant egg at its centre, they are scared – but not nearly as scared as when they discover that the egg is just about to hatch...

The Headmaster's Ghost by Sam Godwin
Danny's school trip would be great if he wasn't being bullied by Adam and Melissa. They try to scare him senseless with stories of the evil headmaster's ghost who is said to haunt the building. Then one dark night, Danny accepts Adam's dare to prove that he's not scared, but it brings more than he bargained for...

All these books and many more can be purchased from your local bookseller. For more information about Tremors, write to: The Sales Department, Hodder Children's Books, A division of Hodder Headline Ltd, 338 Euston Road, London NW1 3BH.